Zavarr Wilmshurst

Ralph and Rose

Faith's defense - a poem, in four parts

Zavarr Wilmshurst

Ralph and Rose
Faith's defense - a poem, in four parts

ISBN/EAN: 9783337089498

Printed in Europe, USA, Canada, Australia, Japan

Cover: Foto ©Andreas Hilbeck / pixelio.de

More available books at **www.hansebooks.com**

Ralph and Rose;

or,

Faith's Defense.

A Poem.

IN FOUR PARTS.

BY

ZAVARR WILMSHURST.

NEW YORK:
CRICHTON & COMPANY, PUBLISHERS,
221, 223 & 225 Fulton Street.

1879.

CRICHTON & Co., PRINTERS, 221, 223 & 225 FULTON ST., N. Y.

THIS

LITTLE BOOK

IS

INSCRIBED

TO THE

CHURCH OF CHRIST,

WHEREVER FOUNDED,

WITH

PROFOUND LOVE AND REVERENCE

BY

THE AUTHOR.

PART FIRST

SPRING.

SPRING.

ORDINARY MIRACLES.

I. .

Earth every Spring is born again,
   And Eden rises from her tomb;
While Love melts Beauty's icy chain,
   And weds her in a world of bloom—
Sun, flowers, stars, and cherubs shedding
Their souls in rapture on that wedding.

   Away, cold reign of rigor!

   Welcome youth, sport, and vigor!
The forest throbs with sighs and cooing,
   And twittering, warbling, fluttering rush:
The very air is given to wooing,
   And kisses every maiden's blush
And dewy, glowing, ruby lips
That her twin rows of pearls eclipse,

Filling her life with health and soundness,
　　Stealing beneath her white neck's muffling
To soft, warm, throbbing marble roundness,
　　　　And, at a saucy parting,
　　Her head of sunny ringlets ruffling.
　　　　At this all-joyward starting,
The gentle gladnesses revive,
　　With freshest fragrance, hues and songs,
And, in Spring's laughing sunshine, wive
　　To fill the earth with fairy throngs.

II.

The greatest wonders are the nearest;
　　The loveliest flowers everywhere;
The treasures we should hold the dearest
　　Are cheapest to our thought and care:
The grandest truth is most neglected;
　　Life's meanest prize man's proudest boast;
Of all the joys by him neglected,
　　Eternal bliss is spurned the most.
　　　　*　　　　*　　　　*　　　　*
Are these antitheses of sages
　　Affecting contrasts and wise gloom,
Or the experience of the ages,
　　Whose truth will stand the crash of doom?
　　　　*　　　　*　　　　*　　　　*

That common things are most astounding;
    Life's highest prizes those that woo,
And greatest blessings most abounding,
    Are truths forever old and new,
Which we should publish, chaunt and cherish,
    Lest in the memory they die,
For countless human millions perish,
    Like blind men, with salvation nigh.

III.

Ha! comes of ghastliness the form,
    Withered like blanched pine, lightning cleft,
Or hoary wreck of sleety storm,
    Long outside of existence left.
Behold the aspen trembler pass
In age's totter o'er Time's glass,
Gasping and shrinking from the blast
As his next moment were his last!
Why does he still the daylight haunt?
Because Death shuddering cries "Avaunt!"
'Tis Winter, father of distress,
The shrivelled slave of cold and barrenness.

IV.

What marvel follows glad and bright,
And lovely as the birth of light?
The year turned young and heavenly fair,
Like rosy child with golden hair,
Nestling amid earth's blossomings
  Where only angel joys allure
And only sweetness breathes and sings,
  Drinking delight as fresh and pure
As from God's fount it gushes clear
Ere mingled with a sigh or tear,—
Spring treading on old Winter's heels
With living green and love-song peals,
And bounding in the pulse as high
As hope that lifts the spirit to the sky.

V.

Though Age grow young again to tell
The thousandth time this miracle
Which sereness with fresh blisses drowns
From deep vales to bald mountain crowns,
Whelming with wealth of sweet surprises—
As joys' throng in the soul arises,
Caught from death's shades which most appal

To heaven's glorious festival—
It will as dust to life compare
With that grand miracle I next declare.

VI.

Gaze with thy spirit on the soul
Who loves the darkness like the mole,
And ever grubs in earth for pelf,
And turns all heart and thought to self;
Who thinks all goodness weak and vain,
Unless it turn to sordid gain;—
The highest wisdom deems to be
His own successful trickery,
And holds his life's and glory's prize
Some shrewd old friend to victimize.

VII.

Heaven of grace has boundless stores
But none for him who self adores—
To whose bleak being loving glow,
Sweet Pity's thrill for want or woe—
Bliss—pain—hope—fear—ne'er find access
Save for his own dear littleness—
Whose lust and greed and hate would urge
To darker crimes did not the scourge

Of man and law his malice check
To save his lucre or his neck:
What can you do with such a knave
You scorn to crush, despair to save,—
Humanity's monstrosity
Masked in external decency,—
A wintry soul, a heart of ice,
Without one virtue or one generous vice?

VIII.

But Grace, although the gentlest power
　　Born of God's love to man,
When he must face his darkest hour
　　And fellest danger scan,
Proves mightiest, even in the strife
Which endless Death and endless Life—
Like tides that clash and foam and roll—
Wage for possession of the soul.
In holy league with Providence,
That right arm of Omnipotence,
Grace watching sleepless in her part
To melt and win the human heart,
Never omits the moment true

The greatest sinner to subdue,
To lead him contrite to her throne
To trust in Mercy's God alone.

IX.

The wretch we drew is born again!
 What else could cleanse so vile a clod,
A nature change, so foul in grain,
 Into the likeness of his God?
Make one whom countless crimes defiled,
Pure, meek and trustful as a child,—
Drive the black legion from his breast,
And render love divine its guest,—
Take Winter from his soul away
And fill it with the bloom of May,—
Turn him from self-idolatry
To deeds of bounteous charity,—
Transform his spirit lost so long,
Into an angel fair and strong,—
And earth, that led to hell's abyss,
Into the threshold of eternal bliss?

George's Adventure.

X.

With monotone and bagpipe drone
　Are bees the woodland flowers lulling,
While George sings merrily alone,
　A busy rifler beauties culling.
'Tis sweet to hear the infant lisping
　The soul of April, May and June,
With voice as free as breezes crisping
　The brook whose song-sighs join in tune,
Wrapping in murmurs his joy notes
As leaves bright flowers in cool moss coats:
The words are all his sister Rose 's;
The air just what his heart composes.

The Song of Spring.

1.

"Spring is coming in its beauty,
　Buds are stealing forth to view;
Nature wakes to life and duty,
　Drenched with sunshine and with dew:
Let us take the sweet example
　Of the hosts that bloom and sing:
Heaven has ever freshness ample
　Souls that love to clothe with Spring.

2.

" Mark yon little peering flower,
  Trembling in the Zephyr's arms!
How she pays back sun and shower
  With the richness of her charms!
Wondrous far her breathing reaches
  That our souls with fragrance feeds,
And the while as sweetly preaches
  ' Make earth lovely with your deeds.'

3.

" Through the wood the wild bird trilling
  With but trees and rocks to hear,
E'en to burst his heart is willing,
  If the waste his rapture cheer.
Let us from his song deriving
  For the soul a guiding spark,
Never cease from noble striving
  Though there be but God to mark."

XI.

His arms and bosom flowing over
  With choice love-breathing, dewy tints,
George marks his pathway through the clover
  And wild ways wilder fancy hints,

With the sweet rainbow wealth he squanders,
As from the beaten track he wanders,
Whence he hath vowed not to be tempted
Till Rose comes back with basket emptied
For the relief of widow Bland,
And homeward they can saunter hand in hand.

XII.

His surfeit has the urchin taken,
And now he seeks the path forsaken:
Chill is the clutch of his dismay
To learn that he has lost his way.
His wanton joys are drowned in fears
And April smiles in April tears:
Troubled his face as rosebud blenching
From its first thunder shower's drenching :
He runs and calls and further strays
As echo with his fancy plays,
And leads him through shagg'd darksome
[walks,
As those through which Death homeward
[stalks,
All ending in a frightful bed
With rocks and blasted trees o'erspread,
Like some inferno all outworn

And 'e'en for demons too forlorn:
An adder springs up in his path,
And hardly has he 'scaped its wrath
Ere a gaunt wolf before him flees
Till in the lone stray child he sees
A delicate and welcome prize
Which he devours with hungry eyes,—
As ice-breathed Winter in retreat
Turns back to blast an April sweet.
" Rose ! Rose !" George shouts as terrors seize
His senses and life's currents freeze.

XIII.

That morning Ralph woods, hills and glens
Roams in keen search of specimens—
Hungry for stones and ores and weeds
On which omnivorous science feeds—
Such as the million would contemn
But each to him a precious gem,
Kindling a flame that doubt consumes
And nature's heights and depths illumes
With light of light till sings this hymn
His heart in logic of earth's seraphim.

DESIGN.

1.

"On everything in heaven and earth
I mark a stamp divine,
Revealing Him who gave it birth;
What is that stamp? Design.
Whether it sprang an hour ago,
Or grew some million years,
The hand that made it well I know,
For there his stamp appears!

2.

"Let skeptics seek the first great cause
In Nature's boundless mine,
And give hard names to all her laws;
What proves them blind? Design;
Whose traces to a child reveal
Truth love joys most to know,
The impress deep, the Maker's seal
Is there God's hand to show.

3.

"No sages can that stamp efface
From aught in earth and skies;
On atoms and on suns each trace
Their reasoning defies:

The simplest floweret breathing sweet,
Clods bearing golden grain,
And man himself, a world complete,—
All, all God's stamp retain.

4.

"Yet not in fragrance of the flower
Or stars on midnight's brow,
Or mountain's height or ocean's power,
Or warbling birds, dost Thou,
O'er charms and miracles of sense,
Thy gracious presence prove
So clear as in thy Providence
And hearts Thou breakst with love."

XIV,

Ralph heard a piteous cry for help,
Which shrilly through the old wood rang;
As lioness to save her whelp
He to the infant's rescue sprang.
'Twas George, the wolf's pugnacious prey,
Grasping his little pocket knife,
And standing manfully at bay,
To save or dearly sell his life:

At sight of Ralph with well-plied staff,
The boy's despair, in triumph's laugh,
And lowering death as quickly sank
As spectres in the churchyard dank
When sun gush swallows gloom: the beast
Fled his anticipated feast
As, met by faith and prayer's defense,
The devil flees from innocence,—
With looks of flame in tremor sunk
And quickly in the thicket slunk.

XV.

Catching the boy up in his arms,
   Ralph kisses his hot tears away;
Freed from the torture of alarms,
   His heart leaps up elate and gay,
And his red pouting lips exclaim,
   'Mid dimpling laughter's overflow,
"How lucky for the wolf you came!
   He did not stop to thank you though."

"You rogue," cries Ralph, "I am a sinner
To rob his Grimness of a dinner:
With mischief you more hearts will rack
Than he and all his prowling pack.

You scrap of spirit lightning cast
Like Eros, born to bless or blast
E'en with your cherub looks and charm
Which would Suspicion's self disarm,
Frail hearts, but yet not mine beguile,
Although a sister in your style,
Some ten years older, well might be,
If we should meet, my destiny."

XVI.

"Oh, you mean Rose. Hark! 'tis her cry."
The urchin shouted in reply.
Soon Ralph beheld a shape of air
With bounding step and streaming hair,
Like angel truant nigh too late
To enter heaven's closing gate,
Or Love that must o'ertake or die,
Or, with the classic strain to vie,—
Like wood nymph from the amorous breeze
In panting flight among the trees.
Now down the rocky glen she flies
Like Rescue swooping from the skies
With lightning in her limbs and azure eyes.

XVII.

Breathless the beauty ends her race
And stands before them with the grace
Of life's love form, fresh, sweet and pure,
Making heaven present, near and sure
And Ralph's heart her delighted slave
In love unbounded by the grave,
And growing of its bliss so fond,
Fancy could dream of naught beyond.
"Oh, George!" she cries, "you heartless elf,
How dare you stray and lose yourself
In woods roamed by the loup-garou
Who feeds on wicked boys like you?
When hunted to this glen he ran—"

"Why, Rose, this is the gentleman,"
Said George, presenting Ralph, with look
Arch and demure, and then he shook
With all the wantonness of glee,
    Like song dance of a bubbling rill,
Or bird from cage in Spring set free,
    Till even Rose, against her will,
The music of her laughter blent
With Ralph and George's merriment,

Just as the flower that quaffs
Morn's golden beaming influence,
When birds their jocund songs commence,
Unbosoms to the sun
Till in her heart he glows and laughs
And steals the sweetness of her soul:
So Rose gave way to George's fun
And crowned the triumph of the droll;
And Wolf's Gorge, as they called the glen,
Was turned to frolic gladness then,
As if it had been Flora's bower
When she smiles love on every flower
And every song re-echoes song:
Though but an instant's gleeful glimmer,
It filled that lair with rapture's shimmer,
Like laughing chaunt heaven's hills among
Of spirit bigots doomed, awaking,
Not in the deep for him bespoken
Of endless death,
Because he scorned their Shibboleth,
But where fresh joys are still creating,
In golden chain,
By dullness, sorrow, care or pain
Eternally unbroken,

New heavens in hearts in meekness deep,
Loving in deeds God's Word to keep,
And room for higher blisses ever making.

PART SECOND

SUMMER.

SUMMER.

I.

Summer to Rose, in splendor dread,
In vastness of all surfeit spread,
Bounty omnipotently shed
From God's great golden fountain head,
O'er valley, brookside, hill and plain,
In waving herbage, fruit and grain,
Making food life an ocean main,
Heaves like a flood that cannot tire,
Or loving Beauty's bosomed fire,
With growing plenteousness until
The founts and wells of blessing fill
And overflow, and Rose o'ercome,
Finds her thanksgiving awed and dumb
At Summer's huge extravagance
Till her good angel breaks the trance
And gives her bursting heart this utterance:

SONG OF SUMMER.

1

" Now the year is in its glory,
    And the sun reigns in his strength,
Earth unbosoms all the story
    Of her boundless love at length,
Hidden during Winter's coldness,
    Timidly revealed in Spring,
But responding now with boldness
    To the kisses of day's king.

2

" Oh what rich and precious treasures—
    Once in Winter's icy hold—
What a host of bounding pleasures
    He unlocks with key of gold !
How their pulse and blushes deepen
    In the Summer's glowing arms !
How her love and breathing sweeten
    Even Earth's most ancient charms !

3

" Starved and frigid was her fairness
    When her breast was clad with snow;

By the sun redeemed from bareness,
  All her veins with blessing flow
That her children all may flourish
  On her bosom's warmth and food,
As our souls still Christ must nourish
  With his precious life and blood.

4

"So the soul once given over
  To the selfishness of sin,
When it finds in Christ its lover,
  Fain would heaven on earth begin,
Burning to bestow on others
  All that can their good increase,
And make men a band of brothers
  By the might of love and peace."

THE SAGE'S WOOING.

II.

"I never shall forget Wolf's Gorge
And how I found Ralph there," said George,
"In lair so lonesome, grim and fell,
Like star seen in a deep dark well.
Where is he now? What makes him stay?
Perhaps, Rose, he has lost his way

In desert vast or forest brakes,
For even I have made mistakes."

"What would you, child?"
                    "No friend forsakes
A friend."
                "For him you would go forth
Who East from West or South from North
Can hardly tell, and leave me here,
Lone, unprotected!"
                    George's tear
By Rose with laughter's trill and ring,
    While to her heart the boy she presses
    And overwhelms him with caresses,
Is scattered with a sparkling fling,
Like dewdrops by a zephyr's wing,
For though she revels in a freak
That serves his vanity to pique,
She joys in his conceit's excess,
To mark such sparks of nobleness.
"Fear not for Ralph," says Rose.   "To err
    In ways of earth he is not prone:
Too oft the great philosopher
    Misses the path to Heaven alone."

"How can he miss his path on high
Who every star knows in the sky,
Or fail of welcome in a sphere
He always spreads about him here?"

III.

"Ah, George, Ralph has your heart ensnared,
  And taught you too this high flown strain!
For old men boys I never cared,
  And wish you were all child again.
Ralph's uncle gave his mind at first
A quenchless scientific thirst,
And though as yet it is not cursed
With unbelief, I fear the worst.
The soul that close to matter clings
  And o'er its secrets ever pores,
May paralyze the glorious wings
  With which to faith and Heaven it soars.
Strange that this uncle burns to blast
  Ralph with his learned skepticism,
And his pure soul from Heaven cast
  Into Doubt's hopeless black abysm!
And love with eager trust must ache
That he whose thirst God's fountains slake,

Can ne'er for Doubt's dark deep forsake
The gospel's everlasting springs
Of cure for evils earth life brings
   Which clustering throng or madly mope
Till snap at last life's mortal strings,
   And soars the soul in faith and hope,
Beauty and bliss past all imaginings."

IV.

" Why here he comes!"   George shouted
                                       " Who ?
Ralph ?"
             " Not Ralph, but his uncle Hugh."
" What can he want ?"
                      " He was, you know,
Made widower a week ago."

" Six months, child."
                  " Well, a millionaire
For such a trifle need not care :
And if in age he seeks a mate,
Will he grow younger, if he wait ?"
    *   *   *   *
As George steals out with waggish air,
Enters the stately Hugh St. Clair.
The gray-beard blandly smiles to scan
No hindrance to his darling plan,

Which his senescence durst propose
Of gathering the beauteous Rose,
For he the freshest sweetness chose
To bloom beside his snow and blight:
So George had harped his hopes aright.

V.

How cunningly the fox untwines
The skein that wraps his heart's designs,
With flatteries to Rose applied
About her fitness to preside
O'er a vast fortune and dispense
Its income in beneficence,—
Of course not leaving unexpressed
His love, devotion and the rest,—
While Rose with eyes that light her work,
And smiles which in her dimples lurk,
Her needle plies, till ends his glose
Of compliment and in plain prose
His hand and wealth he offers Rose
As grandly as a king his crown.
Blushing she puts her sewing down
To meet his steadfast steel blue eyes
And with deep warmth and calm replies:

VI.

"Thanks for your generous intent!
Deeply I feel the compliment
From one whose learning I respect
But yet"—

         "To what do you object?"

"Not to your fortune, though aware
Wealth gives a wider stage to care;
As Heaven's steward, let my charge
For my small skill be not too large;
Not to your years, for how can they
Cause an immortal soul's decay?
Though schooled by time, by sorrow wrung,
The noble soul is ever young:
But to my girlish fancy (why
My heart's convictions now deny?)
Our marriage views are sundered so—
I say not which are high or low—
That they would need, however fleet,
A million years or more to meet."

"You judge me quick"

         "That I could do
But from the way you came to woo."

" I grieve my manners do not suit."

"They are perfection absolute
I own, but we in heart and soul,—
In their least throb, in their grand whole,—
In all we feel, love, will or think,.
As fire and ice, as snow and ink
Are opposite."

And so they looked,
And if such contrasts can be brooked
In marriage, then come chaos back,
And stretch May on December's rack
Of ice: if Hugh and Rose may wed,
Then let the living clasp the dead;
Let light wed night, or upward driven,
Let black Gehenna marry Heaven.

VII.

He seemed an iceberg wafted South
Into the Summer's spicy mouth,
And his long, snowy beard and hair
Brought into mind a polar bear,—
While she with whom he would be merged
In wedlock, was as fresh a thing
As God e'er made in Eden's Spring,

His loveliness to show and sing;
　And calmly, firmly, sweetly urged
"On discord's shore we should be wrecked;
You are a giant intellect
Whom faith in no form e'er beguiled,
And I but superstition's child.
You proudly as Goliath tower
And brave—nay more—ignore the Power
At whose feet I like infant cower."

"But may not opposites unite?"

"Never can hearts so opposite
Into that holy union grow
Which I call marriage.　'Tis the flow
Of soul to soul in love kept bright,
Pure, fresh and warm by faith, delight,
High thought, respect, and kindness free
And mutual as the bounding glee
Of playmate hearts in infancy,
O'erflowing with life's melody."

VIII.

"A poet's dream or girlish quest!
What pair were ever so much blessed?"

"My parents—who were paired in fact
Like grand thought with heroic act—
Sweet fragrance with love's hue as sweet—
Beauty with strength in form complete,
High use with pure delight combined,
Or love with wisdom in God's mind."

Puzzled, surprised, yet entertained,
So long her aged guest remained
That when he left, Rose felt relieved,
Yet with a dread her bosom heaved
Lest he by her rejection hurt,
From Ralph his favor might avert,
For Ralph of late was named his heir,
And Hugh must know them soon a plighted
pair.

RALPH'S QUEST.

IX.

The love of truth is wisdom's hire.
The heart of Summer in Ralph glowed;
He felt in all his veins her fire;
And through his soul her music flowed.
Would she not make her secrets known
To one whose love for her was flame,

While scientists as cold as stone
   Were plodding calmly on to fame !
He plodded too as tirelessly
   As any Dryasdust could.bore
To some worm-eaten mystery
   Which modern makes historic lore:
But most he burned to dive beneath
   The secrets science now unseals
And prove the universe the sheath
   Of lightning truth which God reveals,
He gave the search his soul of thought
   And fresh intensity of youth,
And in the cells of Nature caught
   Glimpses divine of inmost truth.

X.

In love and wisdom's own behoof,
From rock beds to heaven's starry roof,—
In burning gem and clod opaque,—
In lightning's dance, snow's floating flake,—
In tiger ocean, lamb-like lake,—
Earth's tranquil sleep and direful quake,—
As made for revelation's sake,
The All-wise God Almighty spake,

In tones which dreamy silence make
Too full of loveliness to wake,
And thunders which heaven seem to take
Dash earthward and asunder break;
In principles which secret keep
  Beyond all microscopic test,
And systems in whose awful sweep
  Infinitude is manifest:
But when with rays so pure he tried
  To break through atheistic mist,
"This light confirms our teaching!" cried
  Each rock-intrenched materialist:
The greatest conquests of his mind
  That gave his name to glory they
Warped from the service he designed
  To their idolatry of clay.

XI.

Sick of contention and disgust
With sapient worshippers of dust,
For peace and rest his spirit yearned,
And to the home of Rose his footsteps turned.

XII.

As Ralph the vine-clad cottage neared
To him by love and hope endeared,
A voice caught Night in her descent,
And filled her deepening extent
Of golden dusk with languishment,
While tears of fond solicitude
The hearer's pallid cheek bedewed
At tones whose dying languor pressed
The heart like light's last tremors in the West.

Rose's Song.

1.

' 'The Rose wooed by the Nightingale,
    With song in starlight hush,
Drank sadness first that turned her pale,
    Then love that made her blush:
All night her cheek with white and red
    Betrayed her tender fears
Till sunlight raised her drooping head
    And kissed away her tears.

2.

" Yet day seemed long and dull and dead,
    Compared with night and love:

She joyed yet trembled when day fled,
  And Dian climbed above.
Alas! the minstrel came no more,
  And night, consumed in sighs,
Seemed like the bleak and barren shore
  That once was paradise.

3.

"She paled and faded—every day
  And night some beauty stole
Till all her charms had passed away,
  Except her fragrant soul:
Wafted at last on angel plumes
  To heaven's blooming sward,
Sweetest of all, she now perfumes
  The garden of the Lord."

XIII.

The song sank tremulous to sleep
Just as the moon began to peep
  Above the Eastern wave,
And just as sunset's gleams died out,
Like mourners lingering about
  A dear one's flower-strewn grave;
The last strains panted—faint and slow,

As fond to stay and loth to go;
But scarcely had they ceased ere woke
　A clearer, bolder, heartier song,—
As sorrow had her fetters broke
　And in her hope and trust grown strong:
Cheery yet plaintive still at times,
Pure, sweet it rang as heaven's inmost chimes.

THE UNFAILING FRIEND.

1.

"I have a friend, a faithful friend
　On whom alone I can rely,
Whose kindness for me has no end,
　For, like his love, it cannot die:
Oft I defeat his loving aims,
　And make his gracious goodness vain,
But soon the truant he reclaims,
　And softens my hard heart again.

2.

"Though often I forget Him, ne'er
　Does He forget me day or night;
When I sink deepest in despair,
　And grow a stranger to delight,

How sweetly does his love draw near
  Its sunshine o'er my woe to cast,
And scatter to the winds all fear
  And fold me to his heart at last!

3.

"Staunch are the friendships which endure
  While we preserve our faith to them,
Though wo-begone we grow and poor,
  And all the world beside condemn;
But thine, O Lord! in blackest gloom,
  E'en when I turn my back on thee,
Proves constant, and beyond the tomb,
  Will bless me through eternity.

4.

"He roams afar who won my troth,
  Nor bids love's golden hours repass,
Nor greets the star once dear to both,
  And should we meet no more, alas!
My heart were ever cast away,
  Christ's feet could I not clasp and kiss
And, like fond Mary, weep and pray
  Myself into his love and bliss."

XIV.

A little morsel of a hand,
    As soft as warm, in Ralph's was thrust;
A little voice's reprimand
    Rose sweet, though meant to be robust:
" How oft, Ralph, must I caution you
    Not to expose yourself as now,
Beneath a heavy falling dew?
    Such rashness I shall not allow:
Come in at once, or I'll call Rose!
I should be sorry to resort to blows."

George leads his captive to his cot
As much contented with his lot
As one who strayed from heaven remains
Although brought back to bliss in chains.

        *   *   *   *

A world of tenderest communion
Created by two hearts' reunion,
Blending in strains as sweetly voiced
As e'er o'er foeman saved rejoiced,
Exalts the life of Ralph and Rose
As lovingly their hearts unclose,
And thoughts ineffable arise
From springs of soul sublimities—

Thoughts on whose seraph wings they range
The universe in spirits' freest interchange.

XV.

Heaven by Earth had been forgot
Long, long ago, had lovers not—
Such lovers as these two—revived,
Where woes and evils thickest hived, .
Its sweetness; and should we confide
The secret piety would hide,
We should confess that he with soul
That scorns its wealth of love to dole
But nobly gives to her whose mind
Mates his in truth and love refined,
In gentleness, sweet manners, taste,
Grace, kindness, bounty free from waste,
Intelligence, wit, cheerfulness,
True meekness never spiritless,
Heart piety and purity,
Devoid of cant and prudery,
And—this should be so very small—
A spice of mischief for them all—
Humor whose sparkles dulness kill
As stars night's gloom with beauty fill,—

Has heaven in his home and breast
  Which God for man created first
As meetest, sweetest, loveliest, best;
  Nor has his fiat been reversed
But still delight supreme conveys
When each his holy law obeys,
And man for woman's well might skip
Archangel's bright companionship.

XVI.

Ralph rest had sought from studious thought
  And bathed his soul in freshness sweet
With which he found the Summer fraught
  While worshipping at Rose's feet;
But still at times his mind recurred
  To deep and scientific themes,
And as she watched his spirit stirred
  With revelation's lofty gleams,
She sympathized with his unrest,
  And wished his faith, like hers, enshrined
Above man's scientific test,
  And thus unbosomed all her mind:

XVII.

"Let not my faith on science hang,
  Or demonstration clear and cold,
No more than on the wild harangue
  Of zealot reasonless as bold.
Spirit alone can spirit view,
  And God alone himself declare,
As he hath never failed to do
  In answer to the soul of prayer.
How vainly godless Science tries
To build her Babel to the skies!
There is, thank Heaven! something still
Which mocks her scrutiny and skill,
And ever will her search defy,
Though noonday e'en to such as I.
The wonders of the lens and prism
Lay bare and nature's mechanism
And fuel feeding fire and force
In small and great, still life's prime source
Her search will ever mocking shun:
True Science and true Faith are one,
And lisping babes in prayer clasp
That source no skeptic e'er will grasp.
The ark of God is in the soul,

Too pure and high for man's control;
My spirit there let God attune
And with my heart himself commune,
For human aid would violate
Its awfulness and challenge Uzzah's fate."

XVIII.

" Rose, scorn not science. In its place
The works of nature's God to trace,
And in his love and wisdom bask,
Archangels have no nobler task:
But as man gropes, he is too prone
To view the field already sown
As growth spontaneous. Each new spark
That lights up process once so dark,
Instead of being humbly taken
As ray which should more awe awaken,
As God dispensed with wins acclaim,
To make the spirit quench the flame
That lights its inmost depth divine,
And for clod life God life resign.
This is the soul's forbidden fruit,
And fatal still is its pursuit,
Leading us on, from link to link,
To types upon creation's brink,

And filling us with vanity
And glory of discovery,
While tracing Time's trail from a past
Sublime, illimitably vast,
Embracing life's and nature's fount,
Which tempt the Maker's throne to mount
And boast how deeply science delves
To prove how forms and worlds create them-
selves.

XIX.

"Look not dismayed, my pretty Rose,
For Faith its might to battle owes,
And truth and error conflict wage
Within our souls from youth to age,
And as mankind in wisdom grows
Truth wrestles with far subtler foes.
No longer on the rack or stake
Are we made martyrs for her sake:
The strife grows keener, higher far,
For intellects conduct the war:
The Great-Hearts of our faith now deal
With foemen worthy of their steel;

But he who turns to God for light
And in God's strength maintains the fight,
Can scorn the scientist's surprise
That whelms with mingled truth and lies
And matter's glaring evidence,
The would-be soulless slaves of sense;
For to the seeker never yet
Did God refuse his lamp to set
In his creation which displays
His hand in all his works and ways,
And makes the sky and earth and stream
With his design and glory beam.

XX.

"The strife of all is,—Which the winner
Shall be, the outer life or inner?
The light of sense? or light of soul
Illuming God's and nature's scroll?
The palpable that scoffs at doubt—
As burning noontide, thunder's shout,
World-centre-piercing, cloud-girt rocks,
Earth's herds, infinity's sun flocks
Grazing along the milky ways,
Making us faint with wonder's daze,—

All through the telescope that blaze—
All through the microscope that raise
Eternal marvel and amaze?
Or that more wondrous infinite
The soul, by which alone is lit
The universe to sense and thought,
Without which all that is were nought,
Or mere encumbrance and a mass
Of death, but through whose sun-fires pass
Earth's clods and into beauty melt,
As forms of love and wisdom felt,
Proving God's breath divinely burns
In us and dust to glory turns?
Such is the strife.   Leave me not out
With cravens making it a rout.
As free to choose I hold it right
That soul in soul should fight its fight.
Heavens hallelujahs chant, hells hiss
As cleaves the soul its way to bliss.
The image and the likeness too,
This soul life war, of His who slew
With agonies of agonies,
To which his pangs of flesh were ease,—
All our heaven-barring enemies:

And he against whose spirit's poise
Swell sirens' strains, beat demons' noise,
And shower the shafts of unbelief,
Who closer clasps Salvation's Chief,
Shall win in heaven a place and name
Above the martyrs of the rack and flame."

XXI.

" I am, Ralph, but a simple girl,
Shocked by discussion's flash and whirl,
But sometimes words will come as though
Lightning had set my soul aflow,
Because my faith in God is born
Of love too perfect not to scorn
All proof and confirmation less
Than Christ and his own loveliness;
For in his beauty's every line,
So purely, lovingly divine,—
In every ray of his I see
The proof of his Divinity;
In every word of his I feel
The God no science can reveal.
I dwell not on his All-efficience,
The glorious proof of his Omniscience,

And other attributes that stun
With boundlessness all minds but One;
Nor even on the God of Law
Who fills my mind with dread and awe,
For my heart welcomes most the dove
Of meekness, sweetness, goodness, love,—
(Though comfort whispers in our breasts
All power beneath his softness rests,)
Who came from heaven but to cure
The ills of life and make us pure;
Who turned from greatness, pride and wealth,
From beauty, learning, joy and health,—
To serve the helpless of our kind,
The crippled, deaf, dumb, sick, and blind,
And preached the gospel to the poor,
And led the lost to heaven's door;
And thus he grew our hearts so near,
And to our souls than life more dear.
He lived but love, but mercy breathed—
    Which his last gasp for whom besought?
His death, which endless life bequeathed,
    Ah! can it fill the sinner's thought
With love's all beautiful excess
Of agony to save and bless,

And beckon up atonement's road
Our tottering steps to God's abode,
And not make life a hymn to Christ,
In boundless love imparadised,
While God in him our hearts confess
With rapture's tears of thankfulness?
Proofs, linked like suns in golden chain,
Of such a God seem but profane;
And blazed such proofs from earth to skies
As sense or science ne'er denies,
Which skepticism as madness scout,
My eyes would close to shut them out
As giving me no choice to make
Of faith in God for his dear sake;
For if his beauty, goodness, love,
Grace, mercy, sweetness do not prove
Christ Lord and God, I care not, I,
For all the proofs that learning can supply."

PART THIRD

AUTUMN.

AUTUMN.*

ROSE'S PERIL.

I.

What is that love resembling hatred,
  That selfish, merciless desire,—
Which, like an altar dread and sacred,
  Consumes its victims in its fire?
Ah! Love at least should be protection,
  Nor view its object but as prey;
Yet Claude has sworn, since his rejection,
  His loved one and himself to slay.

*   *   *   *   *   *   *

Now through the lattice fiercely gazes,
  The savage, hither crept in stealth,
On beauty which his senses crazes—
  Rose breathing sweetness, grace and health,

---

* The four parts of this poem, "Spring," "Summer,"
"Autumn," and "Winter" are thus entitled because each
part was written at the time of the year after which it is
named but all four were intended to be suggestive rather
than descriptive of the Seasons. The alternative title,
"Faith's Defense," should also be taken with similar
limitation, as the author, far from attempting to cover
the whole field, has contented himself with indicating a
plain and noble line of defense.

Singing in pure affections' tones
That into cheer lull Autumn's moans,
And harkening murder melt in strain
Sweet as glad news by which despair is slain.

SONG OF AUTUMN.

1.

"Autumn's golden tresses weighted
    With the riches of the year,—
And her lap with plenty freighted,
    Ripened brown and purple cheer,
With abundance fraught and sated
        For all life and health and mirth,
        Make her heiress of the earth.

2.

" Gorgeous Autumn hath imparted
    All the wealth we can employ,
Which when garnered well and marted
    Turns bleak Winter into joy.

3.

" Wisdom ripe that Age hath mated—
  Sorrow's priceless riches—life,
Noble deeds have consecrated—
  Heart in love still young—and strife,
Which from the soul hath alienated
  Every littleness and pelf,
  Make Age heir of Heaven itself.

4.

" Flesh in Death's hour well may tremble
  At the pit so dark and grim,
But the souls that Christ's resemble
  Death nor grave can keep from Him."
Here seems to end the golden links
Of her sweet tones, but as she sinks
Her head on her dead mother's chair,
Murmurs her song as if in prayer :—

5.

" If a noble heart is bleeding
  From a wound mine bled to give,
Let—at angels' interceeding—
  Peace and sweet forgiveness live
Up the heavenward pathway leading,

Till his soul its grandeur wakes
And the spell of passion breaks.

6.

" If through me must come an anguish,
   Let no other suffering bear ;
If for me his pleasures languish,
   Give him, Heaven, all my share !"

II.

No flower that highest angels cull,
Breathes tenderness ineffable
So mightily as softly awed
Rose's last tones the soul of Claude :
Though low as death, their depth sincere,
As heaven's blue intensely clear—
Sunlight of perfect love's God sphere —
Revealed to him a goodness vast
From which his spirit shrank aghast.
Trembling he stole from the dear spot,
Shrinking from self as from a blot
On nature, nor e'en durst he raise
His eyes to meet that Heaven's gaze
That scorched his soul : In haste he fled
To woods that densest darkness shed.

REMORSE.

III

Natures that cower but to force,
Could ne'er have suffered Claude's remorse;
Nothing so deep and keen could live
Save in a heart most sensitive;
And Claude, in danger bold and proud,
By Virtue's awfulness was cowed
Because his mocking scorn scarce veiled
Worship profound that never failed
Beauty in Goodness to discern
For which love's heart must ever yearn,
And inmost thought to subjugate
To Virtue pure and delicate;
For though wild passion's stains it bore,
His soul was noble at the core.

IV.

Beings in Nature's grand accord
   Find her a mother rich in gifts,
Though some are loved and more abhorred
   As thought or mood or passion shifts:

In springtide's sun Claude's soul had laughed
  Till wanton with delight it grew;
But now late Autumn's gloom it quaffed
  Where thickest shades their horrors brew,
And there in his moroseness sunk
Of self-created woe grew drunk.
It soothed his mind at life to growl
And hear the winds of heaven howl;
To echo sighs that Nature heaved
As of their charms the storm bereaved
Her ladened trees and bosomed vales,
And scattered them in whooping gales:
His heart said "Even Nature grieves
And weeps o'er me her falling leaves,

While swift-winged hosts her skies forsake
And to her heart creeps every snake,
For she her breast all bare must strip
To Winter's keen and icy grip."

V.

Wearied at last of dreams so foul—
  Of dragon snaring snowy doves,
Of glaring wolf and hooting owl,
  And hell's own hideousness which loves

Its horrid shapes in minds to flaunt
  On which the clouds of conscience lower,
Bright Cheer, that child of Heaven, to daunt
  And turn e'en Christ's sweet pardon sour,
Claude's spirit rose.   A Father's call
From heaven reached the prodigal,
And wrath at self less wildly surged,
And into light his soul emerged,
Still cumbered with some shadows sad
Till to his bosom leaped a lad,
Exclaiming, "Claude! has luck forsaken
Your sport or are you ague shaken:
You look half dead and buried.   Fie!
You should be happy as am I;
For you are noble.   My heart owns
That but for you my little bones
Would now be rocking 'neath the sea
Instead of dancing on your knee.
I love you, Claude, and I can tell
Another who loves you as well."

  "Who is it, George?

          "Blanche Arlingsted

Worships the ground on which you tread.

She's pretty too and sweet as Rose,
And has a hundred handsome beaux.
I pity her, for keenest woe
Is love despised."

       "What do you know
About it?"

       "All: I'll tell you Claude,
(But do not let it get abroad)
I once had Cor, a pretty bird,
The sweetest singer ever heard,
That flew into a fluttering rage
Whenever I went near its cage,
Although I tended it with care;
And yet it loved that Ralph St. Clair,
Coming and wooing at his call.
This was enough to raise one's gall,
And once I felt my bile so stirred
That I resolved to kill the bird.
I see you blush for me.   Poor Cor!
We men have much to answer for."

VI.

" Where is Ralph now, George?"
        "In a war
Of words at Beechhill.   It is bad

To talk too much. He drives me mad,

When I would speak. Why, Ears and Eyes,

Not Tongue, Rose says, make people wise.

I left his company and dull

Discussion on the beautiful

With ladies and his uncle Hugh—

What is the hour, Claude ?"

                "Almost two."

"Then I deserve the soundest rating.

Good-by, dear Claude, for Rose is waiting."

VII.

George sight outleaped as wild birds vanish

   That hear the erring fire-arm's burst.

Claude smiled; then sighed, yet strove to

                    [banish

   The gloom he had so lately nursed.

He turned his steps to Beechhill Grove,

And on his way his fancy wove

Mixed webs whose lines, like sunless day,

Changed darkness into sober gray.

Now clouds are breaking overhead

As memory draws Blanche Arlingsted

Whose pure white charm and blush attract
The gaze of love, but ne'er exact
A dazzled worship which the dome
Of God befits, but not sweet home,
For, free or forced, it must oppress
A mate whose soul is manliness,
Who on his hearth its god must be,
Or scorn his own authority.

VIII.

With thoughts adrift on smoother tide,
Beechhill was reached, and, at the side
Of Ralph, self-doubting Claude felt safe
From the mad freaks of passion's chafe;
For spirit's curb is spirit higher;   [fire.
Ralph's white heat calm tamed Claude's wild
Ralph played and sang. His golden clutch
Of chords and liquid lightning touch
Flung from the cool piano keys
(As humming bird's wings whip the breeze
Till one but darting swiftness sees)
More sweetness than draw swarms of bees
In Spring from flowers all day long;
And, thus sustained, his mellow song

And voice grew luscious, full and round
As seraph's in whose tones resound
Immortal love, unbounded, sprung
From God,—all ripe yet ever young ,
In thrills of joy, in bliss of tears,
And gathered richness of some million years.

RALPH'S SONG.

1.

"What is the beautiful on earth
   But heaven come below
To lure us to the home of God
   Where none can sorrow know?
The sun all gold, the moon all sheen,
   The stars like angels' eyes,—
The streams that murmur evermore,
   And glass the clear blue skies,—
The flowers that sweetly breathe and blush,
   Like babes in rosy sleep,
Herald that world where none—except
   From joy's excess—can weep.

2.

"The beautiful, the golden chain
　Which Heaven to earth supplies,
The angels twine about the heart
　And lift us to the skies.
A maid with beauty (like the Morn
　Whose blush puts out the stars,
When she the portals of the sun
　With glowing touch unbars)
Dawned on my soul with light as soft
　As fills the courts above,
But Heaven summoned her away
　And left me only love.

3.

" The beautiful is wisdom's form
　And love's, but nothing more,
Which we with their sun life should fill
　Brimful and flowing o'er;
Then as you bathe your soul in light
　Of gentle dawn and eve,—
As beauty's charms your thoughts of all
　But grace and love bereave,—

As dusk's first birth of stars you watch
  And Spring's first roses greet,
Let Heaven make your heart and soul
  As pure and bright and sweet."

BREAKERS.

IX.

The equinox in Autumn rumbling
  Drew Ralph and Claude from dames in silk
To billows white with fury, tumbling
  On rocks and churning their own milk.

"I like," said Ralph, "this wild commotion
  Among the hosts of tireless waves;
I like the winds that lash the ocean
  Until for very wrath it raves.
Mark the long lines of armies crested
  March dauntlessly against the shore,
Until their charge, by rocks arrested,
  Breaks up in foam and battle roar!
E'en while my footing shakes with terror
  And stinging spray flies in my face,
I think of error's strife with error
  On the mind's sea of all our race.

For every moment an opinion
  Rises to sink and disappear,
The lofty struggling for dominion,
  To split on solid facts as here.
Behold the waves of swelling fashion
  By ever shifting folly clad!
Here dashes too tumultuous passion
  In chase of its own ruin mad."

X.

"That last lash, Ralph, on me descended,"
  Said Claude, "and I must own it just;
But passion only has offended;
  If that bids sin, then sin I must.
God made you like yon cliff and I
  Am but the reckless, dashing breaker;
So was I born, so shall I die ;
  And who shall dare arraign my Maker?"

XI.

"Ah, Claude! you flatter me and slander
  The nature God to you has given,
Because you fancy it far grander
  To be all dash and thunder-riven.

Of torrent impulse every feature
   You proudly own but mirrors mine,
And if I am not passion's creature,
   Let prayer be praised and Grace Divine.
Yon cliff whose head is heaven's neighbor,
   Serenely sentinels the sea,
(While foam-lipped waves its sides belabor,)
   Like God's eternal truth not me.
Mark well their headlong onset dashing
   To bring the cliff on their own heads,
And their recoil in wrath and splashing,
   Snow-boiling whirl and flying shreds!
And thus as banded skeptics batter
   Salvation's everlasting rock,
Its might and calm their forces shatter,
   Scatter, confound, o'erwhelm and mock,
Still scathless stands its front serene,
As if such bitter foes had never been!"

XII.

"I like your preaching, Ralph, far better
   Than any other I have heard,
Because you do not reason fetter
   And are as good as your own word;

But I can never tell my loathing
  For that too much professing pack,—
Foxes and wolves that wear sheeps' clothing
  And every noble instinct lack.

    *   *   *   *   *

First comes your bigot stern and wrathful,
  Soul-cramped in creed, yet heaven's pet,
Whose god is but a despot scathful
  To all except the bigot's set.
Next stalks his saintship stiff and formal,
  In his perfection's pride and chill,
With gust quite orthodox and normal
  Except for close and luscious ill:
But worse than either is the weeper
  O'er others' sins his own outweigh,—
The fawning, whining, pious creeper
  Into the trusts he dares betray
In the sweet face of heaven—ay,
Though widows wail and orphans cry
Whom he despoils, and, starving, stretch
Their hands for vengeance on the wretch:
And shall they not God's lightning fetch,
Though still he pray and preach some mission
To raise the heathen souls' condition?"

XIII.

"Claude! Claude! you speak with too much
    gall,
For they are few you set for all.
In battle we fought side by side,
And view that past with worthy pride,
For we fought in our country's ranks
And hosts unborn shall give us thanks.
Than they who with us deathward dashed,
Nobler ne'er steel in battle flashed;
But where sounds War her fife and drum
And draws not round a human scum,
Worse than the carrion birds of prey
And battening on the dead as they?
But though they pestered each brigade,
Could they our holy cause degrade?
And where is he who now believes
That hireling braves and craven thieves
Heroic armies represent
That blood alone for freedom spent;
Or thus would Honor's self defame
And patriotism a cheat proclaim?

XIV.

"And with our patriot hosts accord
The human armies of the Lord
Whose ranks those reptiles still infest
Mercy herself can but detest,—
Skulkers and hucksters, souls like pools
Of filth and loathly as the ghouls,
Who yet with cant all converse spice
To make religion mask their vice,—
Their pride, ambition, avarice,
Lust, meanness, hate, and cowardice ;
But though faith's hosts these miscreants
    haunt,—
The curse of earth's church militant,—
And atheists joining in the plot
The record of the saints to blot,
From Satan's pallet pigments choose
To paint them in his darkest hues,
The pure in heart can they defile,
Or join the holy with the vile ?
With noblest feelings, thoughts and deeds
Onward and heavenward still proceeds
The march of saints of every nation
Led by the Captain of Salvation.

XV.

" The purest gold and noblest gem
That beam in royal diadem
Challenge the counterfeiter's skill
As pure religion's graces fill
The hypocrite with lust to dress
In their meek-hearted loveliness,
The hell within him of deceit
And win e'en heaven with a cheat :
And idiots are they indeed
Who let the heartless knave succeed
His sounding brass as gold to pass,
And make them slight pure gold as brass—
Religion's counterfeit palm off
Till at Religion's self his victims scoff.

XVI.

" The hypocrite who dares pretend
    To own the pearl beyond all price,
The matchless grace its beauties lend,
    Proves as he toils at his device :
If thus the shadow be esteemed
    Think how its glorious substance blessed
Those Christ himself from sin redeemed,
    And godhood on their souls impressed !

Some rose to fame and led the world,
　And others in the ranks remained,
Under the banner Christ unfurled,
　And over sin and selfhood gained
The victory whose crown is set
With morning stars of glory met
To hear the seraphs' joy in song,
As one more mortal joins their throng,
Escaped from flesh and death's decree
To put on immortality.

XVII.

" But though the gems of God imboss
The crown of him who bears the cross
Through Sin　and　Death's　dark　shadowed
　vales,
And the steep height to Heaven scales,
While fiery shafts Apollyon hails,
And with temptations dire assails,—
Let me confess how oft he quails,
And his hard lot and woe bewails,
And though the battle must be won,
In his own might it is not done :

The son of grace is ne'er o'erthrown ;
He conquers, but by Grace and Grace alone.

XVIII.

" The flame of Grace that angels fanned
    To life with gentle wings and care,
In soul imperilled will expand
    Terrific into lightning glare,
Beat Satan back and turn to chill
    By Heaven's chastest, loveliest spell,
The fiercest lust he can instill,
    Born in the firiest depths of hell.

XIX.

" Not only in majestic start,
But in calm home—on busy mart—
Where Love her sweetest treasures hives—
Where Interest her bargains drives—
Where souls expand—where they contract—
In passion's calm and cataract—
In dealings small—each petty thing,
Whether it cheer the mind or sting—
In the far mission where the wild
Outhorrors aught but its own child

In foulest, densest darkness bred
Magic and murder ever spread,
While he who toils to break its reign
Torture defies and your disdain ;—
In sweet refinement's downy clasp
Whose folds oft hide Sin's deadly asp,—
In dire misfortune,—slight mishap,—
In starving want, or plenty's lap,—
Before the world at martyr's stake,—
In secret God alone can break,—
Engirds the soul the flame of Grace
Its strength in honesty to brace,—
Whether attacking or attacked,
And keep it pure in aim in act.

XX.

" But he whose prayer to God is trust
In love as infinite as just,
God—in his dealings best portrayed—
In grace comes ever to his aid,
And is as sweetest mercy felt,
But to the bigots who ne'er knelt
Save in the pride that bows the knee
Less for their sins' impunity

Than place on high, as courtiers wring
By worship favors from their king,
God seems the despot he would be
Were one of them the deity.
But must you kiss the bigot's rod
And worship his idea of God?
What! crush for him your loftiest thought,
And fall beneath his juggernaut?
Better learn faith on Afric's shore
And fetish with its blacks adore!
Clearly in Christ is God expressed,
God in the flesh, God manifest:
Study his life, his steps pursue,
Nor skeptics heed, nor bigot crew,
And he your soul to heaven will build
Till it becomes his palace filled
With forms sublime and blissful air
That breathe his love and glory there;—
Till God's own image Adam bore,
But more divine the Heavens restore;— .
Till doubt is dead and buried too,
And God makes his abode with you;—
Till Christ and you blend into one
As light and fervor in the sun."

PART FOURTH:

WINTER.

WINTER.

I.

Rose, Blanche and George in sport together
  Are making merry with the snow,
With cheeks all rosy from the weather,
  And hearts with gladness all aglow:
And now they have their full of laughter,
  And their mad romp is at the best,
Blanche flies, with her wild playmates after,
  And round the cottage hearth they rest.

II.

"My heart," said Blanche, "has burst its traces;
  To you, dear Rose, the fault belongs;
Charm the steed's leaps to sober paces
  With one of your sweet home-made songs."
"Ah, sport," said Rose, "is grave employment;
  The lightest zephyrs sigh at times;
So we will temper our enjoyment
  With pensive tones and thoughtful rhymes."

Song of Winter.

1.

"Lo the earth hath clad in bleakness
    All her charms dead long ago,
And the sun betrays his weakness
    In a faint and heartless glow:
While he mocks her vain beseeching
    To unfreeze her bosom bare,
Skeletons of trees are reaching
    To the heavens in despair.

2.

"Not a bird is here to chaunt me
    Songs of gratitude and cheer,
But long blasts of moaning haunt me,.
    Filling me with vaguest fear!
E'en the brook that used to battle
    With its pebbles night and day,
Long hath ceased its dulcet prattle,
    Frozen still and hard as they.

3.

"Not a sweet friend now is left me
    Of the throngs that won my love;.

Winter hath of all bereft me
But the sparkling hosts above:
In my soul their beauty burning,
While o'er earth he spreads his pall,
All my soul to heaven turning,
Proves his teaching best of all.

4.

"Other seasons, all indulgence,
Rain their bounties full and fast,
Drowning thought with their effulgence,
Till bare Winter comes at last,
Bidding thought the inmost enter
By the gateway of the soul,
And draw nigh creation's centre,
Life, light, spirit, source and goal."

II.

"Thanks, darling Rose, you charm the senses
With sweetness luscious as love's feast,
And yet your song pure truth dispenses
As grandly as God's chosen priest:
And I need now a fresh imbuing
Of gospel light, lest it go out,
For Hugh St. Clair has been pursuing

My soul with reasoning and doubt:
I am I know a fool to listen
  To learned eloquence I hate,
As is the bird to watch the glisten
  Of serpent eyes that fascinate;
But he begins, all fears disarming,
  On pleasant themes that win the ear;
On Nature wonderful and charming,
  Till his discourse makes her appear
The universal legislator,
  And life the product of her laws,
And, finally, her own creator,
  The first, the last and sole great cause.

III.

"I shrink and sigh as he is showing
  Matter is all that was and is,
And soul or spirit but the showing
  Of some of its chance qualities;—
As hope into the grave is slipping,—
  And soul of its unending term
And godlike grandeur he is stripping,
  To leave man but a writhing worm;—
As angels' beauty, heaven's blisses,
  We trust the righteous will possess

When death their souls from earth dismisses,—
  He sinks in utter rottenness,—
· I shrink and sigh, but as for trying
  To stem his rush of fallacies,
Or even battle by denying
  That he, in his pet theories,
Has shown how first it came to pass
Planets and suns were made of gas—
How matter is the source of all—
How into laws it chanced to fall,—
How blent, how solid made, resolved,
And into higher forms evolved,—
And mind is but its attribute,
And man himself another brute:
Why I, should I such sage depth dare,
As his primordial ape would fare,
Or missing link "—

          " You have me there,"
Cried George. " I once by Hugh's discourse
Was swept so nigh to man's head source,
On learning's scientific sea,
Back to my monkey pedigree,

That when he stopped, I did not fail
To look behind to view my tail "

IV.

" Smother the rosy wag !" cried Blanche,
" George, if my eyes could lightning launch—
Well, I would spare you, but not Hugh,
If he should my Claude interview
As he does me.   It makes amends
That Claude and Ralph are such staunch
                                    [friends.
When we are married, Claude and I
Shall for our faith's defense rely
On Ralph and you, Rose.   Heaven I sue
That at one hour and altar too
We wed—we four.   This afternoon
Hugh will be here.   I shall go soon :
He chills me with his cold gray eye :
But one more song, Rose; then, good bye."

SONG.

CLAUDE TO BLANCHE.

1.

" ' Blanche! beautiful Blanche! a moment delay,
Nor pass like a glorious vision away ;
My heart is like ice and my brain is on fire,
And my hate and my horror will madness inspire,
Unless you remain, like an angel of peace,
And cause my soul's tumult and anguish to cease ;
For how can despair in the spirit find place
That is cheered by the smile of your beautiful face ?

2.

" ' Blanche! beautiful Blanche! ah yet linger awhile !
I am better, much better, but lacking your smile,
I fear a relapse; but I think that the cure
Would be perfect indeed and forever endure,
If your pure little hands you would but allow
To rest for a spell on my feverish brow,
And the light of your eyes to stream through my heart
Till they force the last shade of its gloom to depart.

3.

"'Blanche! beautiful Blanche! I have health once again,
But I doubt, if you go, that it long will remain:
Many care not how seldom their doctor they see;
But mine I would have forever with me;
For I'm sure of good health and pure joy by your side;
So you see, if you love me, you must be my bride.'
Thus Claude urged his suit until 'Yes' she had said,
And the beautiful doctor and patient were wed."

The song's conclusion laughter greets,
While Blanche in sport the singer beats,
And cries "Ah, darling, arch and gay!
How dare you make our hearts your play?
But you shall meet your match. Beware!
Goliath Science, Hugh St. Clair,
Is coming, who will tax your wit."

"For David's part I am not fit,"
Says Rose. "He's apt to fall who boasts:
My trust is in the Lord of Hosts
Who faith sincere ne'er yet forsook:
I'll take my pebbles from the brook
And trust my shepherd's sling will be
A match for Gath's huge brazen panoply."

V.

"Rose, that is fine, but I must go."
"And I," said George, "will be your beau."
"No, George."

      "Yes, Blanche, for Claude shall see
I do not lack his chivalry."
"And if to seize you giant come,
Ne'er fear," said Rose, "you have Tom
                   Thumb."

KING OF FROST.

Into the whirling, freezing air,
Still gazing after the vanished pair,
Rose stood and murmured, "King of Frost,
Grim father Winter, I am lost
Like one storm beaten by thy blast,
And on some desert's grandeur cast,
In awe of voices from thy vast
Of snow eternal, where alone,
Viewless and changeless, stands thy throne,
And thou, wrapped in thy icy robe,
Sitst on the summit of the globe,
And breath'st thy mystery to none,
And bidst defiance to the sun.

    *   *   *   *   *   *   *

Not that I hate or shun thee—no:
E'en thy sharp cold and driving snow—
Thy gales that shout like shrill far foe—
Thy gelid plains o'er dark streams' flow,—
I love, and demon-whistled glees
Through branches bare or snow-bowed trees.
Thy night-long, soaring, falling wail,—
Thy spiteful, bitter, pelting hail,—
And, after hours of gust and sleet,
At morn, thy icy winding sheet,
Dazzling as white in the slant sun's chill,
Glassy, crisp, brittle, hard, harsh,—still
I love, because thy hardships fill
My soul with vigor, firm, calm, true,
Lasting Spring, Summer, Autumn through,
And leaving ever such reserve
Of courage, coolness, strength and nerve,
As fits me for the task imposed
To guard the pearl God has inclosed
Within my soul, his grace to me,—
His faith, love, mercy, which are Heaven's
                                        [key."

THE PRIEST OF REASON.

VI.

Sere as the genius of the season,
  With frozen beard and snowy hair,
The prophet and the priest of reason
  Approached the cottage—Hugh St. Clair.
Responsive to his gentle tappings,
  The hostess sprang, the door flew wide,
And he, stripped of his outer wrappings,
  Was seated at the bright fire side.
After kind mutual enquiring,
  And small talk of the neighborhood,
About the living and the dying,
  Which gratified Hugh's gossip mood,
The rich old savant condescended
  To take with Rose a cup of tea,
And with his formal speeches blended
  Much old time wit and pleasantry.
With skill whose art defied detection,
  In hope to 'scape a long discourse
On evolution and selection,
  Rose fain his merry vein would force,
But on alluding to the Winter
  That ruled the land with icy rod,

She proved to him, alas! the hinter
  Of earth's vast glacial period.
Once on his darling hobby mounted,
  Back to the world unstratified,
Through ages ever more uncounted,
  On wings of thought and science hied
The garrulous geologist,—
Back to the sphere of fiery mist
Of inorganic nebulæ,—
(As those in highest heaven may be,
If not the clustering of the suns
Which into one whole glory runs:)
Whence starting with his molecules,
Hugh builds rocks, water, air and mould,
And earth, without a God, behold,

VII.

Rose smiles at this, but keener grows
While he o'er facts of science throws
Such graphic charm as makes them beam
With life and self-creating seem:
Starting at chaos, or its verge,
Step linking step, until emerge
The noblest types from sources crude,

And God, the First Great Cause, exclude:
Dazzling with rich and varied store
Of Nature's wondrous, boundless lore—
Whelming with marvel and surprise
At processes, to make her eyes
Heedful of nature's life alone
And blind to God as were his own,—
He strives her sun of faith to cloud
And wrap her in a skeptic's shroud,
But through each law and trait and trace
Of nature's process, pace by pace,
Each old and new phenomenon,
Brighter than it had ever shone,
That sun, like God wrought miracle,
Beams clear, pure, loving, beautiful,
Or burns majestic, terrible,
Revealing God's almighty hand
From stellar spheres to grains of sand,
Till confirmation overflows
Of revelation's truth to Rose,
Whose soul thus murmurs its delight
To her own heart,—

     " This Gibeonite,
Who digs so deep and toils so hard,

But serves the altar of the Lord
Unwittingly.   Can he exhume
A truth which Faith will not illume
And—though he aims that Faith to hit—
Transform it into Holy Writ?
How vainly skeptic's nature libel!
The universe is God's vast Bible."

VIII.

Against false doctrines' serpent wreathing
   True faith is strong as Eve was weak;
And harmless proves Hugh's venom breathing
   To Rose's spirit pure and meek:
For shielded by Christ's gospel charm
Faith handles vipers free from harm.
Poison with erudition blent,
Rose turns to Gospel nutriment;
And in the earth Hugh stratifies,
Faith's mirrored spirit world descries:
For matter's changes all reflect
The godlike march of intellect
Since first earth's brooding Architect
Was in the deep of chaos lapped,
And first earth's granite bosom wrapped

In rocky robes, in which are furled
Of wondrous shapes world over world,
Which give us now Time's veil to lift
And through those past creations drift
Whose mounts of fire and earthquake births
Make ours seem flames on cottage hearths;
Whose slime bred monsters brood on brood,
Till planets hid or blasted stood,—
Till glared the sun through mists of blood,
And, climbing high, the moon with dread
Turned white and ghastly as the dead.

IX.

Fancy, forbear! for there was nought
Not in its due gradation wrought.
Long ere rock, hill, wood, nook or den
Had crudest human denizen,
O'er horror order was maintained
And through each new creation reigned.
Still milder grew the earth in tone,
Aspect and type and airy zone:
Still progress led the eons' van
To perfect earth for perfect man,
'Till out of fire, rocks, mist and ice
Arose his balmy paradise.

X.

That earth's grand progress in creation,
   As Hugh each page of nature turned,
But imaged man's regeneration,
   Rose with illumined eyes discerned.
From self's heart granite Grace confronting—
   From sources that all evil breed,
To heaven's portal,—there was wanting
   To Rose no symbol of her creed
That as the earth was long progressing
   Till perfect man its Eden trod,
The soul in grace is onward pressing
   Till it becomes the home of God.

XI.

Hugh labors hard to sap and mine
And turn to laughter truth divine:
Rose's compassion wakes for him
Who with a vision near and dim,
Can pore for flaws o'er God's great boon,
And rail as house dog bays the moon,
At Sacred Scripture which to her
And every other worshipper,

Is that pure fount at which to slake
The thirst for life is thus to wake
To life of such God-beaming grade
As makes the sun's wane into shade,
And grants a comfort that outlives
All health or wealth or honor gives.
His work to do, so void of ruth,
As friend sincere in zeal for truth,
Was Hugh's profession and a sigh
Ushered poor Rose's warm reply.

XII

" My friend ?   A friend in heart would ne'er
My happiness a shade impair,
Or rob me of one solace dear
That I can find this life to cheer.
If you are then all you profess,
What faith is to my happiness
Hearken ! My faith is not so weak
Refuge from any truth to seek :
Unmoved it meets all earthly shocks
And though God's Word all paradox
    And fable you appear to prove;
Though all we see you analyze,
And recreate the earth and skies

Of their constituent elements
By methods nature's self invents,
     My faith in Him you could not move,
Who in His fatherly control
And sweet communion with my soul—
His ceaseless providential care
To save me from life's every snare,—
The constant influence of his grace
     My soul from sin and pride to free,
To make it his pure dwelling-place,
     And crown it with humility,
Renders himself to me as nigh,
As palpable, although so high,—
By all my clearest thoughts reveal
And all I most profoundly feel,
As the firm earth beneath my tread,
Or ever-burning suns o'er head;
But could you make experience seem
And God himself a baseless dream,
And revelation but a fraud
By which the lay are over-awed,
What should I owe you for your pains
And what would be my spirit's gains?

XIII.

" I must confess I ne'er could see
Why man should spurn eternity,
And an immortal soul disclaim,
Its godlike source and hope and aim,
And fondly hug his mouldering clay
And life like insect of a day;
For surely gifts that fleet so soon,
Are more a mockery than boon,
And were there save my. soul intense
Of endless life no evidence,
    I could not doubt that deathless clime,
So worthy of the reach and scope
Of aspiration's prayer and hope,
    More than I could this wish sublime:
But granting that the transient space
In which we run our earthly race
Is all we have, let us the span
Fill with the highest joys we can;
And what is higher than the faith
Which from our childhood to our death,
Suffuses life with hues of heaven
    As sunlight earth with golden rain,

And mingles with our woes a leaven
   Whose hope turns all to joy again?
The life of every day grows dull
   Held a drear pathway to the grave,
But deemed a road to God, grows full
   Of cheer and welcome seraphs wave.
Crowded with perils that appal,
   Life pales at death on every hand,
Yet watched o'er by the Lord of All
   And guarded by his angel band,
I rest serenely and secure
   As on Christ's loving breast asleep,
And this sweet thought my spirit pure
   And grateful never fails to keep.
When enemies and even friends
   On me revenge or malice wreak,
What strength to bear and pardon lends
   The Sufferer Divine and Meek!

XIV.

"When flown are wealth and friends so fair,
   And want and care knock at the door,
The thought that I am Heaven's heir
   Makes me content and rich once more.

In sickness and in pain I pine,
    And hours that creep so slowly count,
But as my mortal powers decline,
    Nearer to God I seem to mount.
To health restored, thank Heaven! my feet
    Wander the fields and woods of Spring,
God's smile in every flower to greet,
    His voice in all birds that sing;
And every beauty of the scene
    All living in his love I view;
From the far mountain top serene
    To the near drop of sparkling dew:
And though I doubt not science sees
    Far deeper than my sight can dart,
It can from fragrance, light and breeze
    Ne'er drink faith's rapture of the heart.

XV.

"But it is not o'er life alone
    Faith breathes celestial rosy breath,
Her softest, grandest charm is thrown
    O'er the sharp pangs and woes of death.
In yonder graveyard the remains
    Of my dear parents now repose,

Where fall the Autumn's stormy rains
    And gather Winter's ice and snows :
A dismal thought it were to think
    That all I loved in them is there;
That Virtue's self stands on the brink
    Of dark and nethermost despair.
My father's grandeur I adored ;
    My mother's sweetness was as dear ;
My faith that both to Heaven soared,
    Is firm as that their child stands here.
Their joys dwarf mine as did their worth,.
    Yet I with mine am greatly blessed.—
Health, affluence and love on earth, .
    And hope of heaven's bliss and rest.
I tell you, friend, when mother died
    Her smile was a celestial gleam :
'The heavens open!' faint she cried,
    And though you slight all as a dream
Which then and still my heart elates.
    Her look of bliss and peace profound,
Told she had entered heaven's gates,
    And angels bright had gathered round.
With tears that parting I recall;
    My tears are my heart's luxury

That only bliss can her befall
Where her soul burns to welcome me.

XVI.

"To dwell on self I am to blame:
    I knew your son, a noble youth,
With lightning rapture in his frame
    And, better far, a soul of truth.
You lost him in his bloom of May—
    Tears! I respect your manly grief,
Yet tell me not he is but clay,
    And own it would be sweet relief
To think, as I think, that your son
    Is no repast for worms but still
A godlike soul ordained to run
    A race whose goals of glory thrill
Immortals with a fire sublime
Ever in life and love to higher climb."

XVII.

Rose paused. His hand in her small twain
She took. He tears could not restrain.
She said, "Forgive, if in my speech
Your wounds of soul I dare to reach,

But tell me frankly as a friend
Who would but for the truth contend,
If I,—who am not fired as you
To add to knowledge something new,—
Such solace, joy and peace of mind
In science as in faith can find.
Do not deceive me! By all dear
To your heart's love, oh! be sincere!"

XVIII.

" Deceive you? Never, gentle Rose!
Nor would I shake your soul's repose:
Your faith as life's best treasure shield;
For science can no comfort yield
Like that you tell with so much heart
Surpassing all the skill of art,
And would my learning could supply
A faith so happy, pure and high—
So child-like—"

　　　　　　　"Ah, still there you hold:
Faith is too simple for the wise;
That truth the Lord in prayer told
In his communing with the skies.

From learning is salvation hidden:
  In faith the boast of pride is dumb,
And only they by Christ are bidden
  Who can as little children come.
Laden with erudition's mass,
  Harder who on that wealth rely
It is through heaven's gate to pass
  Than camel through a needle's eye.
Above the highest, grandest thought
  Which has in art or science birth,
The grace of God cannot be bought
  By all the wisdom of the earth:
Distinct, complete and sole,—aloof,
  Averse from all material sense,—
Alike above disproof or proof,
  Itself alone its evidence,—
The gift of faith the Heaven's bestow,
  In all its attributes supreme,
The only real thing I know,
  For all else sinks in Time's dark stream,
Is all of God and God alone—
  The breath that breathes the soul new born;
In source, in life, in proof his own:
  Just as the sun begets the morn

Without a lamp or torch's aid
　So rises faith upon the soul;
And never yet has one essayed—
　Since circling earth began to roll
Through ether with a human freight—
　The throne of Grace with humble prayer,
Childlike, sincere, importunate,
　For faith God's nearest angels share,
Who has not light from God received,
　Clearer than cloudless sun looks down,—
Who has not in his Word believed
　Freer from doubting's chill or frown
Than he on Sinai ablaze
　With God himself, or Christ's eleven
When he ascended in their gaze
　To glory and his throne in heaven.

XIX

"The man in faith and love who walks
　Grows like an angel near the throne,
For with his God he daily talks
　And thinks his thoughts and takes his tone :
His eyes are opened and his look
　Illumined pierces nature through:

Discrepancies that shade God's Book,
  The stumbling blocks in reason's view,
Vanish, and radiantly unfold
  The types and parables divine
Christ, Moses and the prophets told,
  Which truth from touch profane enshrine,
As sword cherubic in the East
  Guarded life's life with girdling flame:
But Faith enjoys the godlike feast
  To which e'en Eden's bliss were tame,
For it is all the spirit's food,
  And for aught else blank is the Word,
But Faith for every need and mood
  Finds it with endless riches stored:
Yet over all ten thousand-fold,
  That privilége of Faith I prize,
Communion with my God to hold
  Which would turn hell to paradise,
Drawing me ever nearer Him,
  And making all mankind to me,
Although their sins o'errun the brim,
  The children of God's family:
And if we only loved as One
  Loved us and proved our love as strong,

·On this wide world we should leave none
    To pine in misery, want and wrong:
.Such is the faith Christ would bestow,
    Founded in love to God and man,
Which death can only brighter show
    The heaven its love on earth began.

XX.

·"You as a naturalist paint
    All-wise design in nature's realm;
I find in faith nor flaw nor taint
    With earth's Designer at the helm
·Of mind and matter's universe—
    Not in that wondrous article
    Of highest bliss conceivable
    With infinite, eternal stretches
    For earth's poor, sinful, contrite wretches
You in annihilation hearse
·Or sink forever 'neath the sod.
    I clasp that Great Designer's pledge!
While you that Light of light immerse,
    That Life of life, that Soul of soul,
    And Love of love beneath the shoal
    Of science, clinging to the edge,

The cuticle of wisdom, we
  Feel its vast heart within us beat.
This as the fittest work for God,
His grandest, best, we view devout
With pity for the thought of doubt,—
God's image, man, and made to be
Forever and divinely free,
His soul in heaven or hell to steep ,
Yet wooed by Jesus from the deep
  Up, up to joy's eternal seat.
The Great Designer cannot lie
  To his far noblest work, the soul—
Or virtue's faith make false as high,
  And with the hope of heaven cajole,—
Make Good itself a fatal cheat
And spirit's purest war defeat;
    No, no!
  Life cannot Faith forego,
  Which solves alone the mystery
  Of discords merged in harmony,
And makes the universe complete
  In truth's and worth's eternity,
Where wrongs they suffered raptures drown,
And on creation set perfection's crown?"

XXI.

Rose ceased and then her blushes burned,
To recollect how she had spurned,
In long and torrent fluency,   [free.
All pause of thought and words her heart set

XXII.

" Is your oration at an end ?
Demanded her white-headed friend.
"Though my convictions are as rock
They have sustained a greater shock
From your unstudied simple speech
Than from all tomes and pulpits teach,
For in your melting tones and eyes
There seems a message from the skies,
Like that the dawn brings from the sun,
Which entrance to my heart has won,
For in your accents strangely rung
The voice of Ned who died so young,
My darling son, so true and brave,
And not as rising from the grave,
But in the tones with which the boy
Oft sweetly summoned me to share his joy.

XXIII.

"Oh, what a vista opened straight
Of light through heaven's fabled gate,
And bliss on bliss in endless chain,
With loved ones there embraced again!
Heart whispered 'Yes, it must be so,'
But Reason chilly answered 'No!'
Yet why should I your faith dispute,
With heart reluctant to confute?
And I own now I cannot see
A path so clear to victory:
You have half won me.   Heaven compels
Belief while such an angel tells
Its story.   Sweetest Rose, adieu!
Were Christians all as good as you,
The force no heathen could resist,
No infidel or atheist,
Of faith so hallowed with good deeds
And love whose will to bless exceeds
All human power, but works forever
With all the heart's and hands' endeavor;
For while fine precepts gain a score
Noble example wins some millions more."

XXIV.

Farewell to him!   Farewell to Rose!
  And it is not too much to hope
That ere his earthly journey's close,
  His soul in darkness ceased to grope,
And heard his Heavenly Father's call,
  Just as the child forbears to roam
When night's dread shades begin to fall,
  And the heart throbs for love and home.

XXV.

True Faith such Philistines of science
  As Hugh, and e'en of greater might,
May ever smiling bid defiance
  And put with shepherd's staff to flight;
But deadlier foes are they who steal
  Or break into the fold of Christ—
Foxes who rob with prayer and zeal,
  Or wolves whose ragings unsufficed
With Christ's life blood shed on the cross,
  Which made atonement's work complete,
Spurn his full sacrifice as dross,

And Hinnon's murders dare repeat
As they grim Moloch would adore
Whose altars ran with infant gore,
And not the God who sweetly blessed
The children nestling in his breast,—
Whose blood all judgment's claims fulfilled
That not a drop more might be spilled,
Crowning all promise of the past—
God's own blood sacrifice, the greatest, holi-
    est, last.

XXVI.

The curse of Faith and Liberty
Is selfish, deep hypocrisy
Or blind, besotted bigotry.
Religion's cloak and Freedom's name
Nor shield nor gild a deed of shame.
No screen from God the guilty shrouds.
Pray for Christ's coming, not in clouds,
But in your heart. There let him sway,
Not once a week, but every day
In every dealing; and no freak
Of wild fanatic, though he reek
With victims' gore,—no pious cheat,—

No wolf or fox with lamb-like bleat—
No heresy within God's church,
   No learned skepticism without,—
No scandal that the pure would smirch
   And clothe with shame the most devout,—
No Pharisee in ice and state,—
No sanctimonious reprobate,—
No spirit world and mediums' drill,
Miraculous and puerile,
Shall shake your faith, forever fed
With God's own truth, your daily bread,
Or you from those high duties swerve
Which God and man and virtue serve
In love and wisdom which display
God to the soul, for God himself are they.

THE END.

www.ingramcontent.com/pod-product-compliance
Lightning Source LLC
Chambersburg PA
CBHW032103010726
47493CB00008B/2513